For Darrel

First published 2019 by Two Hoots
This edition published 2020 by Two Hoots
an imprint of Pan Macmillan
The Smithson, 6 Briset Street, London EC1M 5NR
Associated companies throughout the world.
www.panmacmillan.com
ISBN 978-1-5098-5882-8
Text and illustrations copyright © Daisy Hirst 2019
Moral rights asserted.

9 8 7 6 5 4 3 2 1
A CIP catalogue record for this book is available from the British Library.
Printed in China
The illustrations in this book were created using pencil,
chinagraph pencil, black ink and a computer.

www.twohootsbooks.com

Daisy Hirst

HAMISH
takes the train

TW🦉 HOOTS

Hamish and Noreen liked to watch the trains.

"But where do they go?" asked Hamish.
"To the city," said Noreen.

"Oh, Noreen, don't you
wish we could go and see?"
asked Hamish.

"No," said Noreen.

"But don't you want
to ride in the train?"
asked Hamish.

"No," said Noreen.

"But if you think
it's so great, why
don't you go?"

So Hamish went.

He followed the train tracks towards the station . . .

but when he got there, he found out that he needed a ticket, or money to buy one. So he followed the train tracks . . .

. . . all day, until it began to get dark.

Hamish had not found the city, but in a
yard beside the railway full of old trains and
rusting junk, was a little kaboose with lit-up
windows that reminded him of home.

"Hello?" he called, "is anyone in?" Nobody answered.
Hamish put his ear to the door and heard a groan.
"Are you all right?" asked Hamish.

Inside, everything was made of something else - apart from Christov, who had flu.

"I feel so heavy, so cold!" said Christov. "And I'm supposed to go to work in the morning. I work the crane on a building site."

"Christov!" said Hamish, "Why don't I go for you? I'd love to drive a crane!"

Hamish borrowed Christov's hat and his jacket.
He used Christov's ticket to take the train to the city.

"When you get out
of the station," said Christov,
"look up and you'll see my crane.
Then you'll know which way to go."

"Can't you read?" asked Max the foreman, when Hamish explained he'd come to do Christov's job.

Hamish could read, and he looked at the sign.

He had Christov's hat and his jacket, but Christov's boots would have been too small.

Christov had given Hamish some money for lunch.

It wasn't really enough for boots, but Margot did him a deal.

"Right," said Max, "You'll need to
go on up there. Lisa's going to show
you the controls."

The crane was very tall.
"Taller than all the trees
in the wood," said Hamish.
"Country bear, are you?" asked Lisa.
"Yes," said Hamish. "But I really,
really want to drive the crane."

"Well, I
expect you're
very good
at climbing
trees,"
said Lisa.

"Quite good,"
said Hamish.
"But Noreen
is better,"
he thought.

It was cosy in the cabin.

Lisa showed Hamish the levers for moving the crane's arm, and for lifting things up and putting them down.

Hamish worked the crane all day. The next day Christov was still ill, so he came back and did it again.

From the top of
the crane, Hamish
could see the entire
city, and the green and
blue beyond its edge.
He could even see the
curve of the earth.

On the fifth day, a
flock of Canada geese
flew past the crane.
Hamish found
himself shouting,
"Do you know Noreen?"

But the geese didn't answer.

NO HAT
NO BOOTS
NO JOB

STARS ☆ HOSPICE

TH

As it was Friday, Max paid Hamish his wages and said,
"There's a job for you if you want it."

Hamish bought a pizza with some of the money.
He wondered what Noreen would be having for tea.

"So, Hamish my friend," said Christov, who was feeling better, "what do you think of the city?"

"It's brilliant," said Hamish. "But–"
and he told Christov about Noreen.

"I miss somebody too," said Christov, "but he's thousands of miles away. If I could reach him as fast as you could reach Noreen, Hamish, I'd go all the time! Nothing would stop me. You go on and see Noreen."

Hamish did go, in the morning, but this time
he travelled by train.

Instead of walking all day Hamish
found that, once he was on the train,

he was home almost at once,
and running across the fields
calling, "Noreen! Noreen,
I missed you!"

"Yes," said Noreen. "Yes, Hamish, I did that too!"

"So you're going to be a builder?" asked Noreen.

"Maybe," said Hamish, "and I could come home every weekend on the train. But Noreen . . .

"You know when the trains come in the other direction, from the city to our station here?"

"Yes," said Noreen.

"Well, where do they go after that?"

A note from the author

This story began with a bear and a goose, who'd been popping up in my sketchbook for a few years – gardening, disagreeing, doing jigsaws together. I'd decided they lived in a little shed on a hill that I kept walking past. Separately, I thought it would be fun to make a book about trains and cranes and earth-moving machines – but I was very surprised by what happened when the bear and the goose met the trains and cranes.